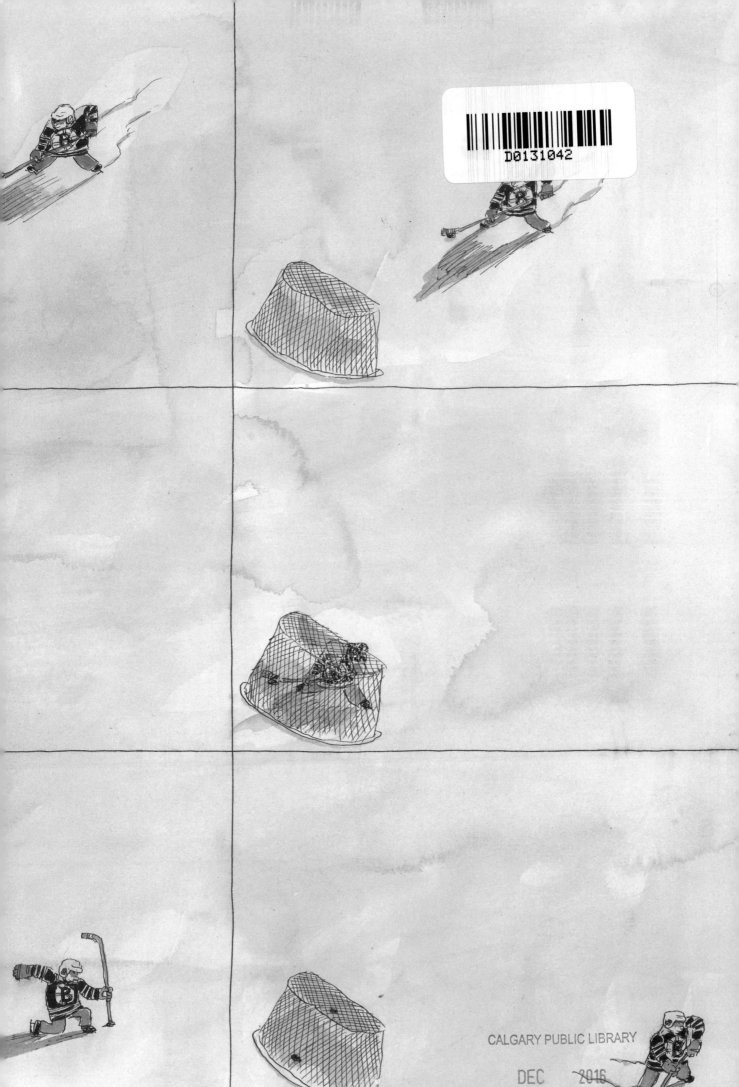

Copyright © 2016 by Greystone Books Ltd.

16 17 18 19 20   5 4 3 2 1

Greystone Books Ltd.
www.greystonebooks.com

Cataloguing data available from Library and Archives Canada
ISBN 978-1-77164-189-0 (cloth)
ISBN 978-1-77164-190-6 (epub)

Editing by Patricia Aldana
Jacket and interior design by Tania Craan
Jacket and interior illustrations by Gary Clement
Printed and bound in China by 1010 Printing International Ltd.

We gratefully acknowledge the support of the Canada Council
for the Arts, the British Columbia Arts Council, the Province
of British Columbia through the Book Publishing Tax Credit,
and the Government of Canada through the Canada Book
Fund for our publishing activities.

Canadä

Greystone Books is committed to reducing the consumption
of old-growth forests in the books it publishes.

THE HOCKEY SONG

BY STOMPIN' TOM CONNORS

PICTURES BY GARY CLEMENT

GREYSTONE BOOKS

Vancouver / Berkeley

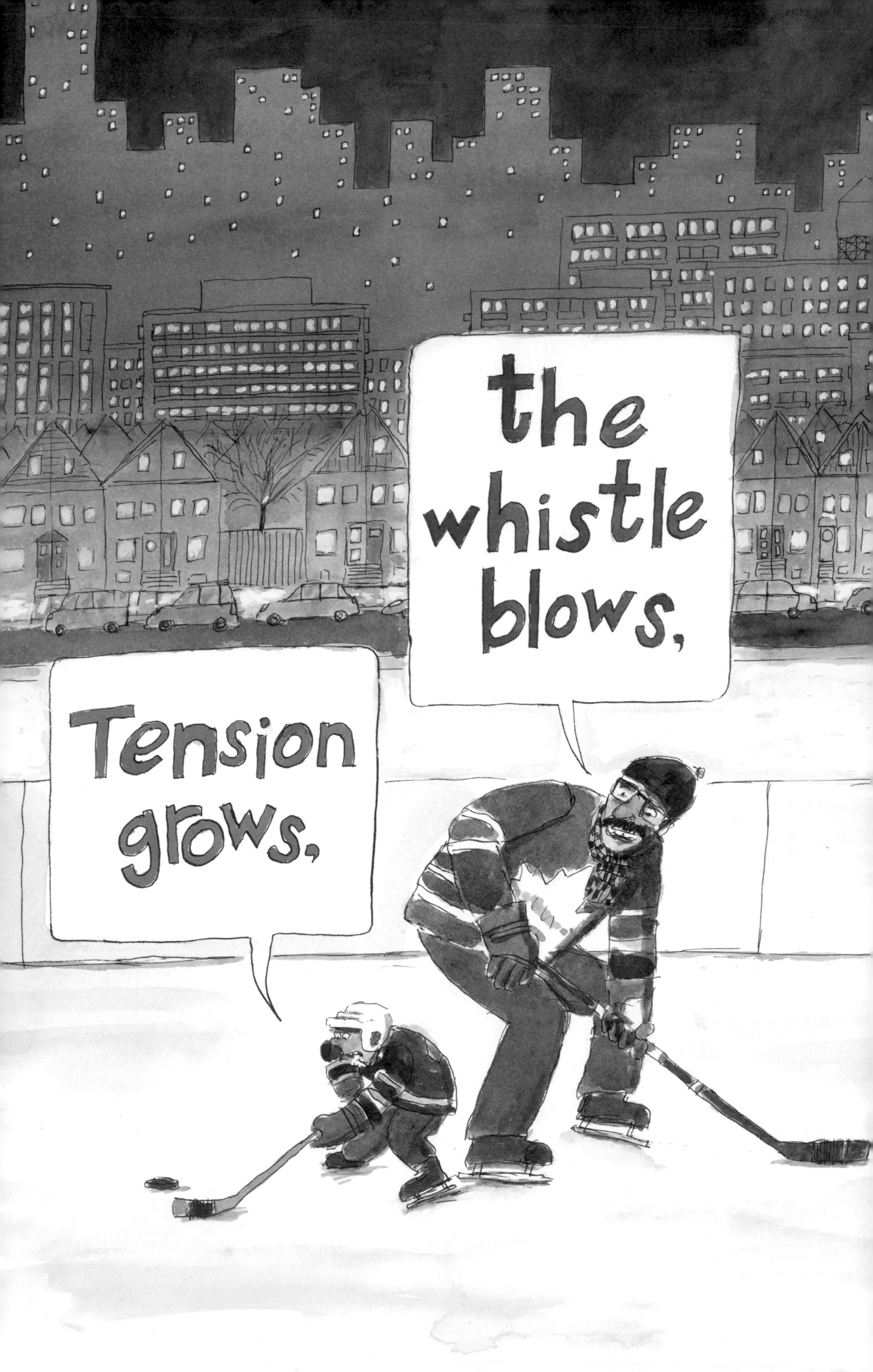
the whistle blows,
Tension grows,

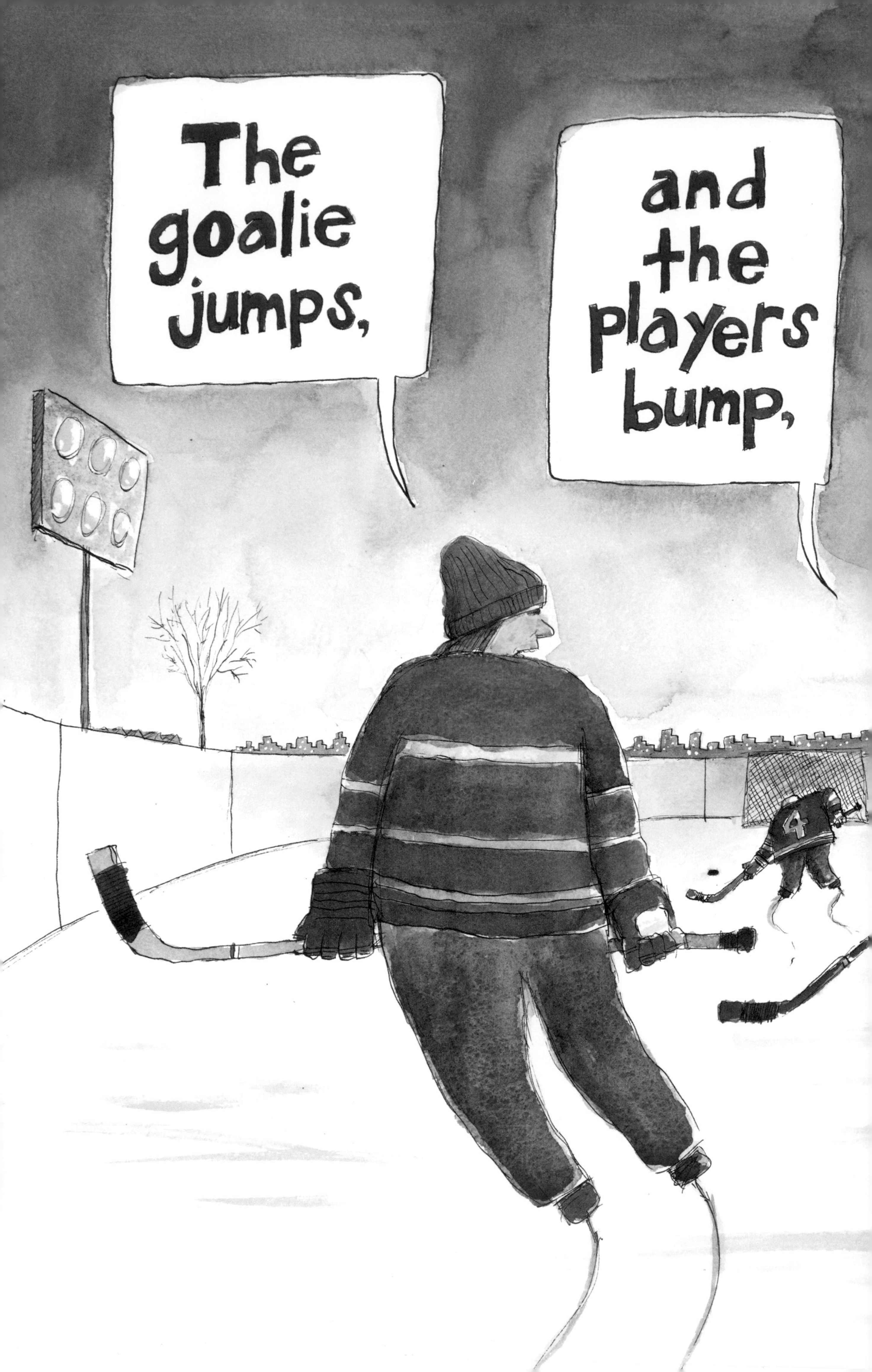
The goalie jumps,
and the players bump,

ol' hockey game,
you can name.

game you can
the good ol'
game.

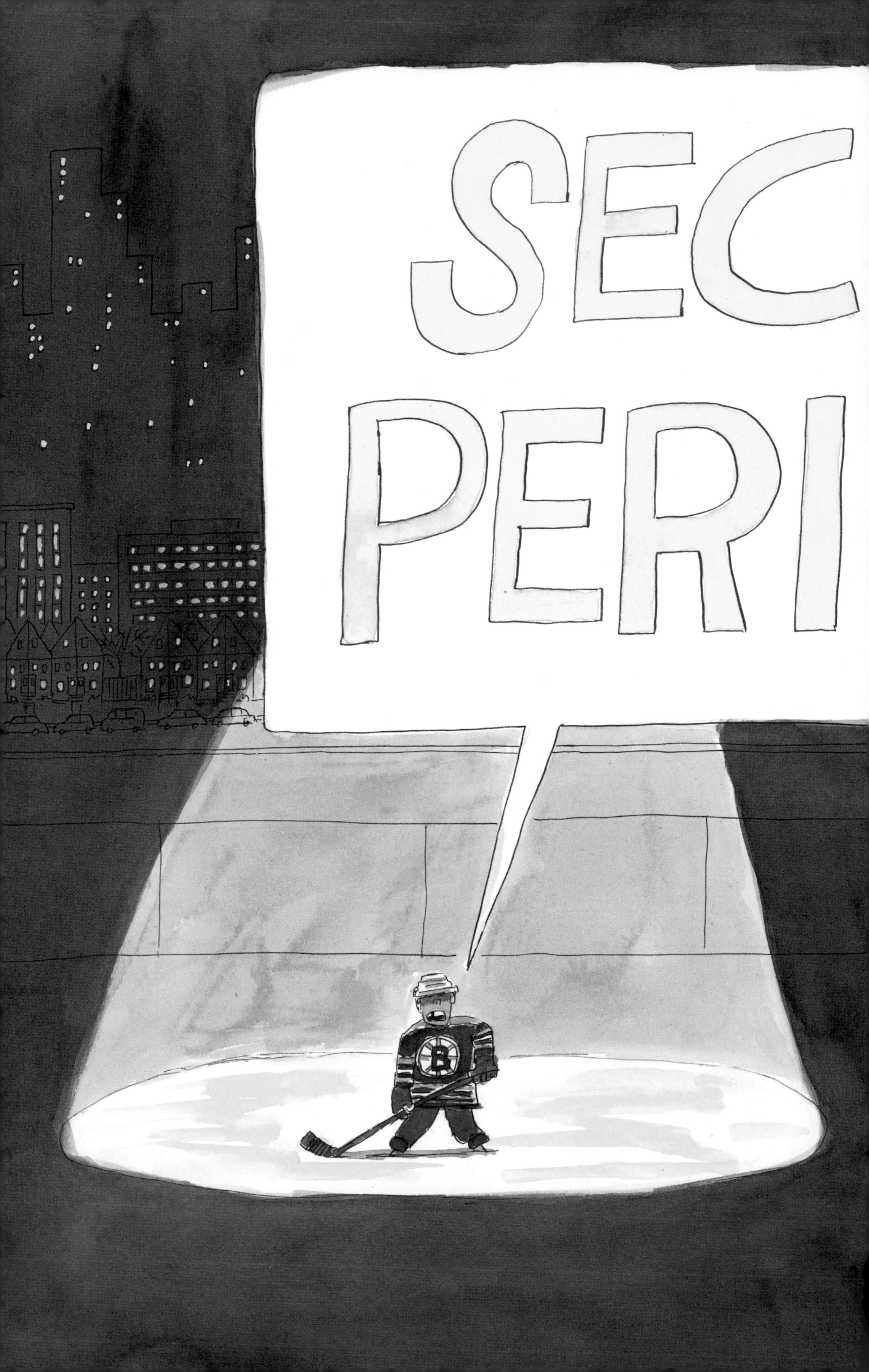
SEC
PERI

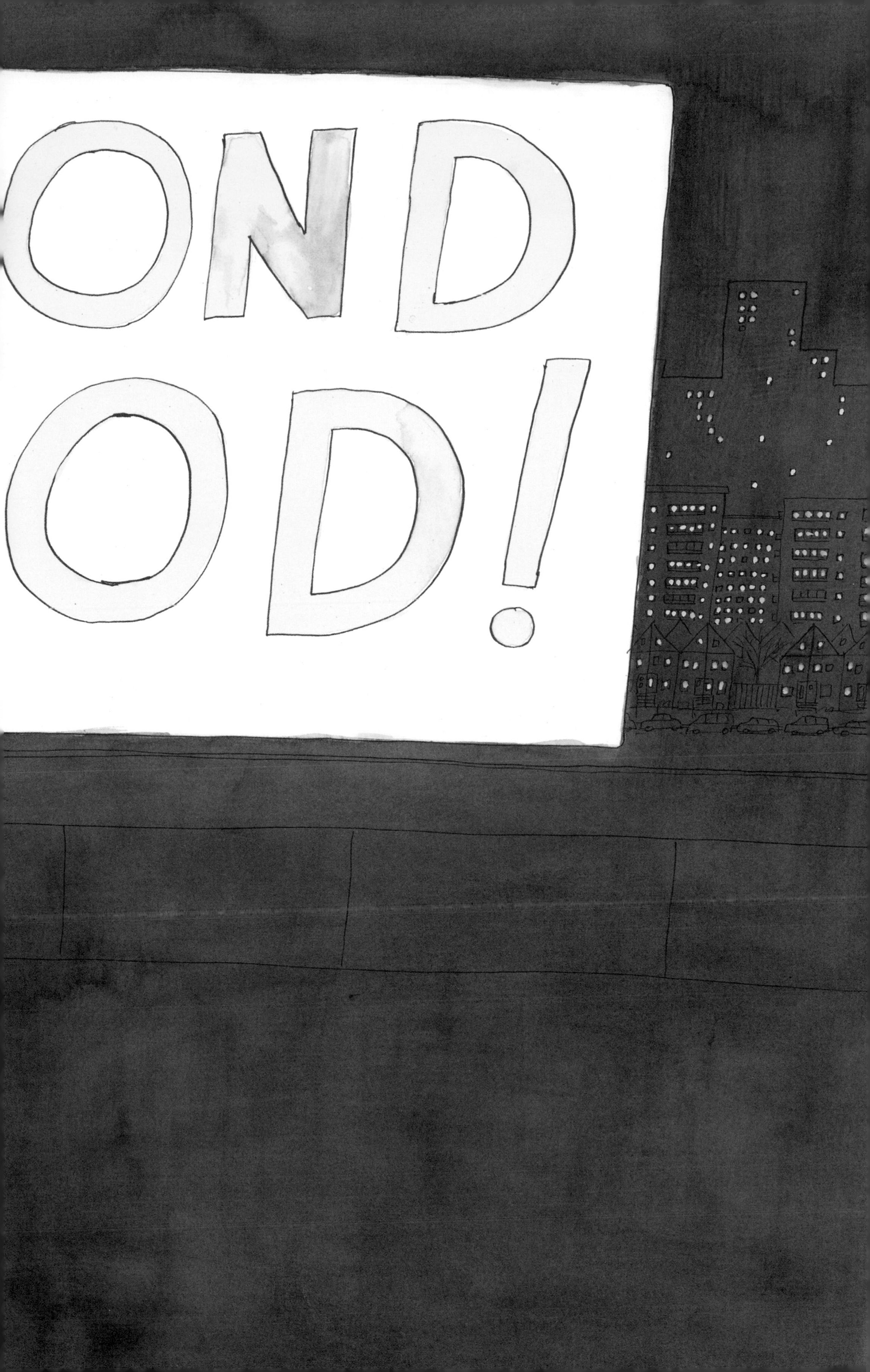
OND
OD!

And the best game you can name, is the good ol' hockey game.

Third period.

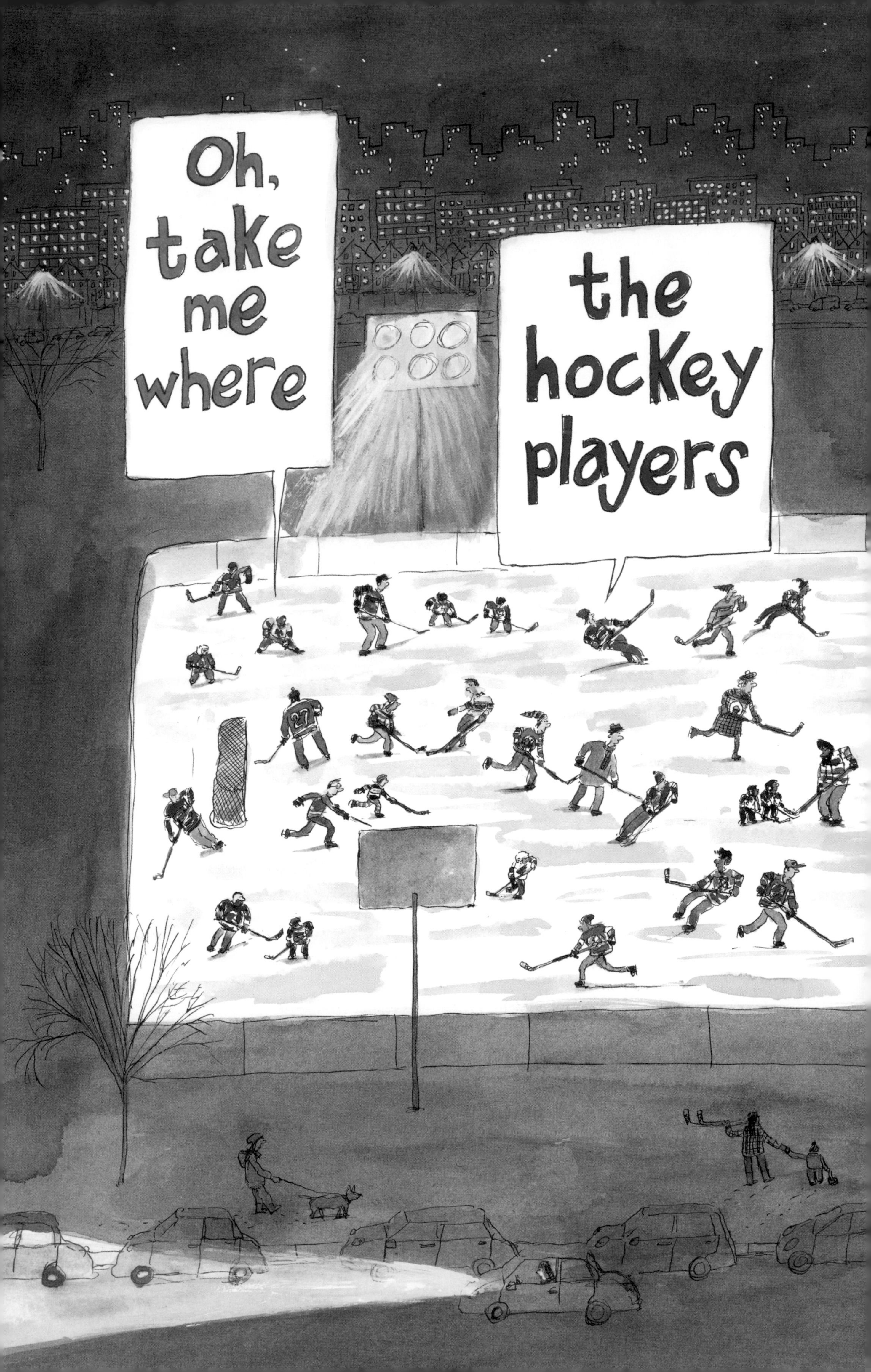
Oh, take me where
the hockey players

good ol'
is the best
name. And
you can name,
hockey game.

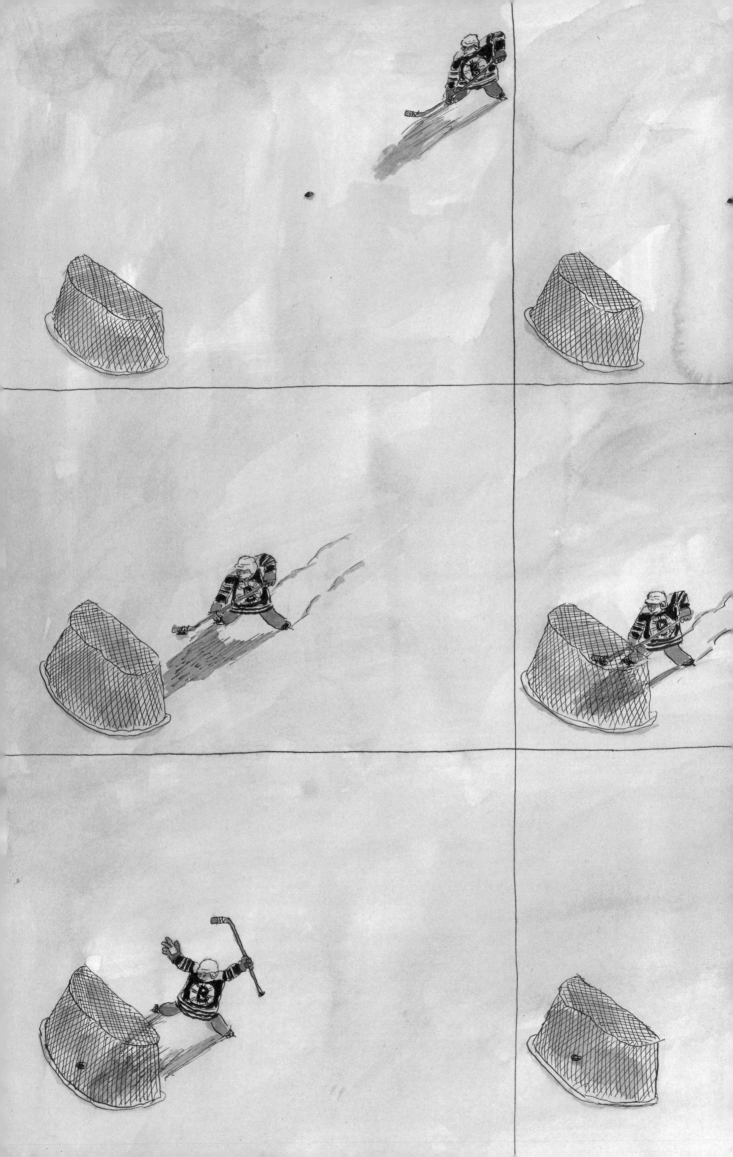